Stripes the ~~Cat~~ Tiger

Written by Jean Leroy
& Bérengère Delaporte

Illustrated by Bérengère Delaporte

Peter Pauper Press, Inc.
WHITE PLAINS, NEW YORK

For Marie, special envoy of the Leroy family in Belle Province
J.L.

For my dad who made great purrs
B.D.

Stripes the ~~Cat~~ Tiger

Stripes is the fiercest
hunter in the jungle . . .

. . . well, actually,
that's what Stripes would *like* to be.

Stripes is a small tabby cat,

just big enough to sharpen his claws on the couch.

Sometimes Stripes' shadow allows him to imagine he's big . . .

... but his reflection
always reminds him that he's little.

Stripes is stubborn,
very stubborn.

When you pet him,
he no longer purrs...

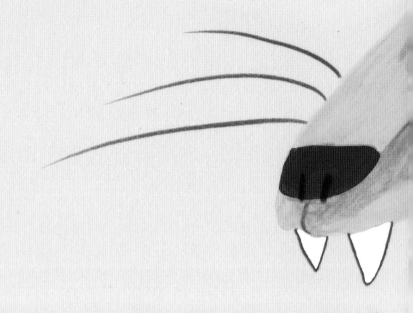

...he ROARS!

He doesn't concern himself with chasing after mice anymore.

He prefers larger prey instead.

One day, his owner had had just about enough of his pretend nonsense.

He decided to take Stripes to the zoo
to see a *real* tiger.

And for the first time
in his life . . .

"Oh wow!" thought Stripes.
"How awesome it must be to be a tiger—
to roar and scare the visitors at the zoo,
eating raw meat in front of frightened children.
That's my ultimate dream-life!"

"Ahhh," thought the tiger.
"How delightful it must be to be a cat—
napping on the couch,
someone to pet me behind the ears,
not having everyone stare at me all day long.
That's my ultimate dream-life!"

Suddenly, both felines
had the same idea.

And from that day on, Stripes became the fiercest tiger in the land, astonishing visitors with his mighty roar!

While the tiger happily purred
all . . . day . . . long.

First published in Canada as *Le chat qui voulait être un tigre* by Éditions Les 400 coups,
Copyright © 2010 by Jean Leroy and Bérengère Delaporte
First published in English in 2016 by Peter Pauper Press, Inc.

English edition copyright © 2016 by Peter Pauper Press, Inc.

Published by Peter Pauper Press, Inc.
202 Mamaroneck Avenue
White Plains, New York 10601, USA

Published in the United Kingdom and Europe by Peter Pauper Press, Inc.
c/o White Pebble International
Unit 2, Plot 11 Terminus Rd.
Chichester, West Sussex PO19 8TX, UK

Library of Congress Cataloging-in-Publication Data available

ISBN 978-1-4413-2184-8
Manufactured for Peter Pauper Press, Inc.
Printed in Hong Kong

7 6 5 4 3 2 1

Visit us at www.peterpauper.com

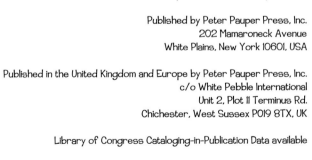